LOVE YOU
TO DEATH

LOVE YOU
TO DEATH

GAIL BOWEN

RAVEN BOOKS
an imprint of
ORCA BOOK PUBLISHERS

Library and Archives Canada Cataloguing in Publication

Bowen, Gail, 1942-
Love you to death / written by Gail Bowen.
(Rapid reads)

ISBN 978-1-55469-262-0

I. Title. II. Series: Rapid reads
PS8553.08995L69 2010   C813 .54   C2009-907244-0

First published in the United States, 2010
Library of Congress Control Number: 2009942217

Summary: Successful late-night radio call-in show host Charlie D
must discover which of his longtime listeners is killing
other members of his loyal audience.

Orca Book Publishers gratefully acknowledges the support for
its publishing programs provided by the following agencies: the
Government of Canada through the Canada Book Fund and the
Canada Council for the Arts, and the Province of British Columbia
through the BC Arts Council and the Book Publishing Tax Credit.

Design by Teresa Bubela
Cover photography by Getty Images

ORCA BOOK PUBLISHERS
PO Box 5626, Stn. B
Victoria, BC Canada
V8R 6S4

ORCA BOOK PUBLISHERS
PO Box 468
Custer, WA USA
98240-0468

www.orcabook.com
Printed and bound in Canada.

13 12 11 10 • 4 3 2 1

To Kelley Jo Burke, who understands the power of radio and uses it wisely.

CHAPTER ONE

A wise man once said 90 percent of life is just showing up. An hour before midnight, five nights a week, fifty weeks a year, I show up at CVOX radio. Our studios are in a concrete-and-glass box in a strip mall. The box to the left of us sells discount wedding dresses. The box to the right of us rents XXX movies. The box where I work sells talk radio—"ALL TALK/ALL THE TIME." Our call letters are on the roof. The *O* in CVOX is an open, red-lipped mouth with a tongue that looks like Mick Jagger's.

After I walk under Mick Jagger's tongue, I pass through security, make my way down the hall and slide into a darkened booth. I slip on my headphones and adjust the microphone. I spend the next two hours trying to convince callers that life is worth living. I'm good at my job—so good that sometimes I even convince myself.

My name is Charlie Dowhanuik. But on air, where we can all be who we want to be, I'm known as Charlie D. I was born with my mother's sleepy hazel eyes and clever tongue, my father's easy charm, and a wine-colored birthmark that covers half my face. In a moment of intimacy, the only woman I've ever loved, now, alas, dead, touched my cheek and said, "You look as if you've been dipped in blood."

One of the very few people who don't flinch when they look at my face is Nova ("Proud to Be Swiss") Langenegger.

For nine years, Nova has been the producer of my show, "The World According to Charlie D." She says that when she looks at me she doesn't see my birthmark—all she sees is the major pain in her ass.

Tonight when I walk into the studio, she narrows her eyes at me and taps her watch. It's a humid night and her blond hair is frizzy. She has a zit on the tip of her nose. She's wearing a black maternity T-shirt that says *Believe It or Not, I Used to Be Hot*.

"Don't sell yourself short, Mama Nova," I say. "You're still hot. Those hormones that have been sluicing through your body for nine months give you a very sexy glow."

"That's not a sexy glow," she says. "That's my blood pressure spiking. We're on the air in six minutes. I've been calling and texting you for two hours. Where were you?"

I open my knapsack and hand her a paper bag that glistens with grease from the onion rings inside. "There was a lineup at Fat Boy's," I say.

Nova shakes her head. "You always know what I want." She slips her hand into the bag, extracts an onion ring and takes a bite. Usually this first taste gives her a kid's pleasure, but tonight she chews on it dutifully. It might as well be broccoli. "Charlie, we need to talk," she says. "About Ian Blaise."

"He calls in all the time," I say. "He's doing fine. Seeing a shrink. Back to work part-time. Considering that it's only been six months since his wife and daughters were killed in that car accident, his recovery is a miracle."

Nova has lovely eyes. They're as blue as a northern sky. When she laughs, the skin around them crinkles. It isn't crinkling now. "Ian jumped from the roof of his apartment building Saturday," she says. "He's dead."

I feel as if I've been kicked in the stomach. "He called me at home last week. We talked for over an hour."

Nova frowns. "We've been over this a hundred times. You shouldn't give out your home number. It's dangerous."

"Not as dangerous as being without a person you can call in the small hours," I say tightly. "That's when the ghoulies and ghosties and long-leggedy beasties can drive you over the edge. I remember the feeling well."

"The situation may be more sinister than that, Charlie," Nova says. "This morning someone sent us Ian's obituary. This index card was clipped to it."

Nova hands me the card. It's the kind school kids use when they have to make a speech in class. The message is neatly printed, and I read it aloud. "'Ian Blaise wasn't worth your time, Charlie. None of them are. They're cutting off your oxygen.

I'm going to save you.'" I turn to Nova. "What the hell is this?"

"Well, for starters, it's the third in a series. Last week someone sent us Marcie Zhang's obituary."

"The girl in grade nine who was being bullied," I say. "You didn't tell me she was dead."

"There's a lot I don't tell you," Nova says. She sounds tired. "Anyway, there was a file card attached to the obituary. The message was the same as this one—minus the part about saving you. That's new."

"I don't get it," I say. "Marcie Zhang called in a couple of weeks ago. Remember? She was in great shape. She'd aced her exams. And she had an interview for a job as a junior counselor at a summer camp."

"I remember. I also remember that the last time James Washington called in, he said that he was getting a lot of support from other gay athletes who'd been outed, and he wished he'd gone public sooner."

"James is dead too?"

Nova raises an eyebrow. "Lucky you never read the papers, huh? James died as a result of a hit-and-run a couple of weeks ago. We got the newspaper clipping with the index card attached. Same message—word for word—as the one with Marcie's obituary."

"And you never told me?"

"I didn't connect the dots, Charlie. A fourteen-year-old girl who, until very recently has been deeply disturbed, commits suicide. A professional athlete is killed in a tragic accident. Do you have any idea how much mail we get? How many calls I handle a week? Maybe I wasn't as sharp as I should have been, because I'm preoccupied with this baby. But this morning after I got Ian's obituary—with the extended-play version of the note—I called the police."

I snap. "You called the cops? Nova, you and I have always been on the same side of that particular issue. The police operate in a black-and-white world. Right/wrong. Guilty/innocent. Sane/Not so much. We've always agreed that life is more complex for our listeners. They tell us things they can't tell anybody else. They have to trust us."

Nova moves so close that her belly is touching mine. Her voice is low and grave. "Charlie, this isn't about a lonely guy who wants you to tell him it's okay to have a cyberskin love doll as his fantasy date. There's a murderer out there. A real murderer—not one of your Goth death groupies. We can't handle this on our own."

I reach over and rub her neck. "Okay, Mama Nova, you win. But over a hundred thousand people listen to our show every night. Where do we start?"

Nova gives my hand a pat and removes it from her neck. "With you, Charlie," she says. "The police want to use our show to flush out the killer."

CHAPTER TWO

N ova walks with me from the control booth into the studio. I take my chair, and she leans against the desk. "We haven't got much time," she says. "So I'll just give you what I know. The police psychologist thinks that whoever wrote those notes believes you're in love with them and that you're sending them a message."

"Telling them to kill the other callers?"

Nova shifts her body against the desk. These days it's difficult for her to find a comfortable position. "The police psychologist believes that your would-be lover thinks you're exhausted, and that you're crying out for help," she says.

I feel the first fingers of a headache moving from the back of my neck into my skull. "And so I'm sending a message to my would-be lover to murder the people who depend on me," I say.

Nova nods. "That's about it."

"Erotomania," I say. "I'm familiar with the syndrome. Does the police psychologist have any handy hints about how I can get my beloved to show his or her face?"

Nova's laugh is short and dry. "I don't think the police psychologist has listened to his radio in thirty years. We're going to have to play it by ear. The cops will be monitoring our calls. They want to be in the control room with me. I told them that having the boys and girls in blue hover while you do the show will freak you out, and when you freak out, everybody freaks out."

"Except you," I say. "You're unflappable."

"After nine years, I've learned to fake unflappable," Nova says. She glances at the clock on the wall. "Thirty seconds to air. I'd better get back in the control room. I knocked together an introduction. It's on your computer screen."

I pull my chair close to the desk, put on my earphones and adjust the microphone. It's time for talk radio—the place where everyone can be who they want to be. The music comes up. The drummer from the Dave Matthews Band counts the band into our theme music: "Ants Marching." I live for this moment—the moment when Charlie Dowhanuik, the freak with a face like a blood mask, disappears and I become Charlie D, a guy who is cool, commanding and in charge.

The words on the screen are Nova's, but I make them my own. Like everyone in my business, I've created a voice that works for my audience. My radio voice is as soothing

as dark honey. For a guy who fears intimacy, it's surprisingly intimate. The voice
of Charlie D is my armor, and as long as I
can fake it, I'm bulletproof.

"*It's March twentieth, the first day of
spring—the season of loooooooooove,*" I say.
"*The Roman philosopher, Cicero, said that love
is madness. Lovers sure act crazy. We're reck-
less. We forget to eat. We can't sleep. We can't
work. We're consumed by our lover's voice. Her
touch. Her taste. Her scent. Her being. Scientists
tell us that Prozac can cure love, but who wants
to be cured? It's fun up there on the merry-go-
round. But what happens when the merry-
go-round starts spinning too fast, throwing off
the other riders, making us sick?*

"*You are listening to 'The World According
to Charlie D' and we are coming to you live
from coast to coast to coast. Tonight's topic is
Erotomania—the delusion that someone, usually
somebody famous, is secretly in love with you
and sending you signals that reveal their love.*

13

"*Remember the movie* Misery *where Kathy Bates uses a sledgehammer and a block of wood to break Jimmy Caan's ankles because she's 'his number-one fan'? Remember Jody Foster's number-one fan, John Hinckley? He showed Jodie how much he loved her by attempting to assassinate the president of the United States?*

"*What is it about love that makes people crazy? Any thoughts? Ever been called a stalker? Ever been a stalkee? Give me a call. My name is Charlie D. Our lines are open, and we are ready to talk about loooooooooove—craaaaaaaazy love.*

"*While you ponder the question of whether you've ever crossed that thin, blood-red line between love and madness, here are The Police with their anthem to those who love truly, madly and deeply: 'Every Breath You Take.'*"

I turn down the volume on the music. When we're on air, Nova and I are separated by the glass partition between the studio and the control room. Nova's control room is brightly lit, but I like the studio dark. We communicate through hand signals and our talkback microphone. We're like fish in neighboring aquariums, seeing one another but unable to connect. Many times, especially lately when I know she's worried about the baby, I wish I could reach out and comfort her. Tonight is one of those times. As she sits behind the desk with the phone nestled between her ear and shoulder, peering over her wire-rimmed reading glasses at her computer monitor, I know she's frightened.

"Hey, Mama Nova," I say. "Are you doing okay? I can hear your heart beating on the talkback."

She turns to give me a thumbs-up. In the blink of an eye, the thumb disappears and she raises the middle finger of her right hand at me.

"So you're mad," I say.

"Just scared," she says. "But I don't know which finger to use for scared."

"Next time tell me sooner," I say. "I can be scared with you."

Her voice is resigned. "Or you can pull your disappearing act. That's when we all get scared: me, the network and, most importantly, our audience."

I feel the familiar lick of guilt. "I'm not that important to anybody, Nova. If I walked away, the network would have another guy here within a week. Within two weeks, Charlie D would be just a memory."

"You're wrong," she says flatly. "As far as our audience is concerned, you're irreplaceable. Our show works because you make every member of our audience feel as if they're alone with you in their room. When you start to disintegrate on air, they fall apart. And I have to deal with the meltdown. That's when the mail gets scary: FedExed chicken soup, mass cards, panties, guides to aura adjustment and some really alarming letters. I'm not just protecting you; I'm protecting me. We're back in ten seconds—and our first caller is Emo Emily."

Emo Emily is the poster girl for wallowing in heartbreak, and she is familiar territory. "The one who broke into my house and stole all my shoes," I say, and I grin.

Nova doesn't grin back. "Don't blow Emily off, Charlie. Anyone who could discover where you live and crawl in through the basement window…"

"Could murder three people?"

"Find out." Nova raises her hand and points her index finger at me. It's my turn now. I'm on the air, and I have one hour and fifty-three minutes to find a murderer.

CHAPTER THREE

As "Every Breath You Take" fades, I sing along. Nova's right. Our audience is sensitive to my moods. They tell me that when I sing along, they relax because they know I'm going to make it to the end of the show. The day my beloved died, I took off my earphones, walked out of the studio and didn't come back for a year. The people who listen to "The World According to Charlie D" worry a lot that I'm going to give them a repeat performance. I worry about that myself.

You can tell a lot about people from their voices. Words can lie but voices can't.

Emo Emily talks endlessly about heart-break, death, despair and betrayal, but when she says, "Sometimes I think I can't go on," there's a fizzy giggle in her voice. Emily knows that she's going to hang in long enough to blow out the candles on the cake her great-grandchildren will place in front of her on her hundredth birth-day. Our listeners get a kick out of her. So do I. When I greet her on air, my tone is lighthearted.

"Our first caller tonight is one of our regulars. Good evening, Emo Emily. Hey, did you notice that line 'Every Step You Take'? Since you made off with my not-very-extensive collection of shoes, I'm down to my high school Keds. They're getting mighty shabby. Any chance, you'll return my other runners?"

"A man's shoes carry him where he needs to be, Charlie," she says playfully. *"I'm making sure your shoes will be waiting when you realize your destiny is to be with me."*

This is not the first time Emily has talked about our fated love, but three murders have given her fantasy a new and disturbing potential. *"So what are your thoughts about our topic tonight?"* I ask.

Emily loves an open-ended question. *"My heart goes out to anyone who hasn't found love,"* she trills. *"On our break today, some of the other girls at the phone bank were talking about how boring their boyfriends are. They say all their boyfriends talk about is sports and getting drunk. I said you talk to me about everything. You're beautiful…"*

I can't let that one slide. *"You've never seen me,"* I say.

It takes more than reality to clip Emily's wings. She flies on. *"A woman knows these things. You and I are spiritual twins, Charlie D. Since I told you that, for me, listening to Emo music is like listening to the sound of my own soul screaming, you're playing more Emo bands. I've counted. You're not afraid of your emotions—not like that robot Marion with all her boring facts."*

Marion the Librarian used to be one of our regulars. No matter what the topic was, Marion did her research. She made the show smart and thoughtful. But smart and thoughtful doesn't cut it with talk radio's hottest demographic: listeners between the ages of seventeen and thirty-four. They like callers who are fun and crazy. They tuned us out when Marion was on, so the suits at the network told us to block her calls. I missed her. *"Hey, Emily, you know the rules. No slagging the other callers."*

My voice is harsh, and Emily is as contrite as a whipped puppy. *"You're not mad at me, are you, Charlie?"* she asks.

"No," I say, *"I'm not mad. Just promise me you won't do any damage, okay?"*

Her voice quivers with relief. *"I promise. And Charlie D, when you're ready to accept your destiny with me, your shoes are ready.*

I washed all six pairs on gentle cycle, and I put them out in the sun to dry. Every day, I sprinkle them with baby powder to keep them fresh."

The image of Emily kneeling to powder my shoes stabs me. I fear these moments. Our listeners are loyal. They would do anything for me. They offer up their lives, believing I have the answers. Every morning I wake up thinking that this is the day they'll discover the truth. I'm a broken man and a fake. I need to shut out these thoughts when I'm on the air. I'm relieved when Nova tells me our next caller is another regular—Podcast Pete. With Podcast Pete on the line, it's impossible to think about anything.

When I was a kid, my father, in an attempt to turn me into the kind of son he could be proud of, took me to a place that had a batting cage and a pitching machine. That pitching machine was merciless. I tried swinging at the pitched balls, but I never connected. I tried catching them, but they stung my hand. Finally, I just stood aside and let the pitching machine hurl balls toward me, *rat-a-tat-tat*, until my time was up. I never did learn how to hit a ball. I never did become the kind of son my father could be proud of. But I did learn how to handle high-octane callers like Podcast Pete. You just have to stand aside and let 'em rip.

Tonight Pete is flying. *"Enemies, enemies, enemies,"* he says. *"We're surrounded by enemies, Charlie."*

I find my soothing voice. *"Chill,"* I say. *"You're scaring the horses. You're sounding a little—uh—caffeinated. How many Jolts have you had today, Pete?"*

"I lost count. It's immaterial. I have to stay awake. Sleep is for the weak. I've got to stay on top of it. Twitter. Facebook. MSN—got to check with my friends. And I've got my podcast discussion pages—some real ugliness

brewing on the discussion page about our show, Charlie D. A lot of people out there don't appreciate your sense of humor—we've got a fight on our hands."

"My granny used to tell me 'sticks and stones may break my bones, but virtual names will never hurt me.' Let it go, Pete."

"I can't. Charlie, you're an outsider, an outlaw. You don't live by the rules. You're a visionary, and visionaries have to be protected."

Nova and I have always shrugged Pete off, but her face on the other side of the glass is solemn. Through my earphones, I hear her voice. "Push him."

I nod. *"So, Pete, who do you think I have to be protected against?"*

His words are an avalanche. *"Against the ones who are trying to keep you from realizing your vision. They're out there. They're everywhere. Charlie, I download every episode of your show. I fall asleep—well, something like sleep—listening to you on my iPod, over and over.*

Ideas come into my mind. When I get up, I know I have to clear the way for you."

The words form themselves. *"Clearing the way wouldn't mean hurting anybody, would it, Pete?"*

Tense, Nova leans forward against her desk.

Pete sighs heavily, and when he speaks his voice is lifeless. He's starting to crash. *"Sometimes in the middle of the night, I open my eyes and my heart is pounding—like it's gonna pop out of my chest...and eat someone... you know...like in Alien. I think of all the people I have to fight—and I get scared. Then I remember what you told me John Wayne said."*

He falls silent. On radio, dead air is the enemy. *"John Wayne?"* I say.

Pete doesn't respond, and Nova and I exchange glances. After nine years we know how to read one another's signals. Pete has tanked. Ready or not, we have to move to the next caller, but Pete surprises us. It's an effort for him to speak, but he's back. *"It was when I told you that some days I can't face leaving my room,"* he says. *"You reminded me that John Wayne said 'Courage is being scared to death, but saddling up anyway.'"*

For the second time tonight I'm stabbed by the knowledge that for a lot of our listeners, I'm life support. I can't be that anymore. It's tough to keep my voice from breaking. *"Pete, you don't have to fight my battles,"* I say.

Pete's reply is a whisper. *"What else would I do with my life?"* he asks. Then, finally—mercifully—the line goes dead.

CHAPTER FOUR

My headache is worse. The fingers of pain have moved up my skull to press on my temples. Nova has been watching me carefully. She knows I'm not doing well. As if by magic, her words appear on my computer screen. I flash her a smile and start reading. My voice surprises me. As I read Nova's script, I sound like a winner—one of those guys who breezes through life with the wind at his back and who takes no prisoners.

"*You're listening to 'The World According to Charlie D,*'" I say. "*Our topic tonight is*

Erotomania. When we're in love, we're all crazy, but some of us take crazy to a whole new level. The Icelandic singer-songwriter Björk had a persistent lover. He sent her a book that was rigged to blow up in her face. And a video of himself putting a gun into his mouth just before he committed suicide. In my opinion, a box of chocolates and a dozen roses would have been cooler. Any thoughts you'd care to share?"

I give out our call-in numbers and email address. Then I turn back to the words on the screen. Tonight is not a night for riffing.

"When it comes to crazy love, no one is immune," I say. "Even Anne Murray, Canada's singing sweetheart, had her own sketchy swain. Do you remember the Saskatchewan farmer who believed that when Anne signed a fan photo for him with an O and X, she was declaring her love? Her rural Romeo returned the favor by showing up at her door with a bouquet of flowers and a loaded twenty-two. The Barenaked Ladies honored him with a song. Our lines are open."

As the Barenaked Ladies sing "Straw Hat and Old Dirty Hank," I talk to Nova.

"Are the cops listening in?"

"They are indeed," she says. "In their opinion, we're two for two. They think both Emo Emily and Podcast Pete have real nut-bar potential. Officers in their home-towns are on their way to question them as we speak."

"So we betrayed them," I say tightly.

"Charlie, we had no choice."

"Damn it, Nova, neither did they. No one chooses to be screwed up. Our listeners had the bad luck to draw losing numbers in the great lottery of life. Now it looks as if they got another lousy number when they called me."

"Don't beat yourself up," Nova says. "You talk people through crises. You make them laugh. You give them hope. You make sure they have referrals, so they can get the help they need. And more times than I want to think about, you give our listeners your home phone number. You're there, Charlie, and that's what matters."

Nova's voice is small and strained. She cares about our listeners, and she believes in our show. Calling the cops flies in the face of the trust she has built with our audience in the nine years we've been on the air. "It's going to be all right," I say.

"Yeah," she says, "and some day I'm going to wear size zero jeans. Back on in two seconds, Charlie. You'll be talking to Rani—long time listener, first-time caller. She's an archaeologist."

"A student of human cultures," I say. "I wonder what she makes of our rag-tag band of the walking wounded?"

"Ask her," Nova says crisply. The tiny light on my microphone base comes to life. I'm back on the air.

"That was the Barenaked Ladies with 'Straw Hat and Old Dirty Hank,'" I say.

"Our next guest is Rani. Welcome. My producer tells me you're an archaeologist, Rani. That's a first for our show."

Her laugh is deep and musical. *"That surprises me,"* she says. *"So many of your callers are unexplored ruins. You're a magnificent ruin yourself, Charlie D. It would be fun excavating you."*

I relax. The fingers on my temples ease their pressure. Rani is going to be a five-star guest. *"Fun for me but futile for you,"* I say. *"I contain no hidden treasures, Rani."*

"Maybe the wrong women have been doing the digging," she purrs. *"I'm experienced. I know where to look."*

Through the talkback, Nova groans. I hold up my hands in a gesture of surrender. *"Hey, Rani,"* I say, *"you're making me forget these are public airwaves. Time to focus. Our topic tonight is Erotomania: the belief that another person is secretly in love with you and is sending signals that only you*

31

can understand. We've just met, but you strike me as a woman over whom a man might fantasize. Am I right?"

Rani's chuckle is X-rated. "I've had my share of dysfunctional lovers," she says. "They're fun until you want them gone—and then it can be challenging."

"Did anyone ever take it too far?" I ask.

She sighs. "Ah. There was one lover who was…inconvenient."

"Care to share?"

"He was another archaeologist," she says. "We were on a dig at the Giza Necropolis in Egypt."

"Home of the Great Sphinx," I say.

"Do you know the riddle of the Sphinx?" Rani asks.

For the first time that night, I'm in the groove. Talking to Rani is like playing tennis with a pro. "I do," I say. "Which creature goes on four feet in the morning, on two feet at noon and on three in the evening?"

"Do you know the answer?"

Now I'm having fun. *"The answer is man,"* I say. *"He crawls on his hands and feet as a baby, walks on two feet as an adult, and walks with a cane in old age. Of course, I'm still crawling. I plan to stick with it till I get it right."*

Rani's contralto becomes even huskier. *"I find the image of a man crawling toward me...appealing. But no reward for you, Charlie D. You had the wrong Sphinx. The Sphinx who posed your riddle was Greek."*

"Does it matter?"

"Oh yes. If you'd given the wrong answer, the Sphinx would have..."

I finish her sentence. *"Devoured me."*

"You sound eager," she says. *"My lover at the dig was like you—preferred his sex on the... risky side. When that became a bore, I told him to go away...and he wouldn't."*

In the control booth, Nova draws her index finger across her throat. The lines are jammed. She wants me to cut short the fun and games with Rani. I ignore her. I lean into my microphone. *"I understand why your lover wouldn't go away,"* I murmur.

"Do you?" she says. *"Then maybe you'll understand why finally I had no alternative but to seal him in a tomb...with a picture of me...just me and the darkness...This has been delightful, Charlie D. We'll have to do it again."*

It appears our tennis match is over. Rani smashed a ball past me, and I didn't even see it coming. *"Wait,"* I say. *"I've got more questions."* But I'm talking to dead air. She's gone. I glance toward the control booth, but Nova's on the phone, so I carry on. *"O-kay. Looks like Rani went off to dig something—or someone—up,"* I say. *"The topic tonight is Crazy Love. You heard Rani's story. She sealed her too-passionate boyfriend in a tomb. How do you handle a lover who won't take no for an answer? And what if he* or she is somebody you've never met? Give us a call. To get you in the mood, here's a song that honors trapped lovers everywhere: Robert Palmer's 'Addicted to Love.'"

CHAPTER FIVE

The music starts, and I call Nova on talk-back. "That was a trip through bizarro world," I say. "So was Rani just having a little fun with me, or is she really a man-killer?"

Nova's voice is tense. "The police couldn't trace the call. They think she was probably using one of those cheap phones you can buy at convenience stores."

"So my move is to keep charming her on air and hope she'll call back on a landline."

"Or make a personal appearance here at the studio," Nova says. "And you're back on air."

I give it my all. *"Rani, Rani, Rani,"* I plead. *"Why did you hang up on me? We were just getting to know each other. You enchanted me. You bewitched me. And then—you ditched me. Give me another chance, my seductive student of mysterious cultures. I am a ruin in desperate need of excavation."* For the tenth time that night I tell listeners how they can reach us by phone or email. Then I glance at my monitor and read the name of our next caller. It's Britney—another regular. She's young, self-absorbed and sweetly crazy. Britney's sentences tilt up at the end. It's as if, before committing herself to an opinion, she has to see which way the winds are blowing. Despite the winds that are battering me tonight, I try to be a gentle breeze for her.

"Hey, it's Britney, the devil baby," I say.

"Oh, Charlie," she trills. *"You know I'm not the devil baby. I don't even have any real problems. I just like to hear myself on the radio."*

"*Don't we all,*" I say. "*So, Brit, what's on your mind on this first day of spring?*"

"*Orlando Bloom,*" she says. "*Because I'm, like, no longer addicted to him.*"

"*Ah,*" I say. "*So you're a recovering Bloomie.*"

She corrects me. "*A recovered Bloomie. And I was, like, so into him.*" Her words cascade like a waterfall, shining and unstoppable. "*I saw every one of his movies nine times—even* The Curse of the Black Pearl, *and that movie really sucked. When I read on his website that he and the other members of the* Fellowship *got the elvish word for 'nine' tattooed on their wrists, I got the elvish word for 'nine' tattooed on my wrist. And my mother just about disowned me because I used my birthday money. It was supposed to go into my college fund—like I'm ever actually going to go to university.*

"*And I became a Buddhist because Orlando is a Buddhist, and I went green and started recycling everything because Orlando is seriously into caring about the environment. I was like a total Orlando Bloom FREAK!"*

Nova and I exchange smiles. The child Nova is carrying is a girl. Nova believes her daughter will be a Nobel Prize winner. I tell her she'll probably give birth to the next Britney. The current Britney stops to take a breath, and I see my chance. *"So what made you decide to do the Orlando detox?"* I ask.

She sighs theatrically. *"Loving him just took too much time. No offence to your Buddhist listeners, Charlie D, but all that meditating really ate up my mall time. And I'm sorry—I believe in recycling and all, but whenever I stirred my compost heap, that smell stayed in my hair for, like, hours."*

"So how did you kick the habit?" I ask.

"Purging."

I wait for Britney to embroider her story, but she has become a woman of few words. *"Purging as in throwing up?"* I ask encouragingly.

39

"*Right,*" she says, and she's back on track. "*Doing the technicolor yawn. Spewing. Woofing. Zuking. Blowing chunks.*"

"*Got it,*" I say. "*So how do we purge ourselves of the passions that destroy us?*"

"*Condensed milk,*" she says. "*Charlie D, for a man who's supposed to have all the answers, there's a lot you don't know. Every time I thought of Orlando, I just drank a can of room-temperature condensed milk. By the time I was halfway through the second case of milk, I couldn't look at Orlando without ralphing, and I'd lost seven pounds.*"

"*Impressive,*" I say. "*No need for a twelve-step program when you can open a can of moo and chug-a-lug. Keep clean, Brit…*"

I glance into the control room. Nova is talking on the phone, but she's also keying a message on her computer. I look at my screen: Appeal to Rani. Make it good. Then we'll go to music. Marilyn Manson—"Sweet Dreams."

"Hey, Rani," I say. "Are you purging yourself of me? We were getting along so well and now...silence. What went wrong between us? I need to know. I'm waiting for your call. You're my fantasy. Here's Marilyn Manson's take on the love that doesn't quit—'Sweet Dreams.'"

The music starts, and Nova is on the talkback. "No word from Rani," she says. "The coward in me hopes that we won't hear from her again—that she's just vanished, crawled back into whatever hell-hole she crawled out of. Then I remember Ian Blaise and Marcie Zhang and James Washington, and I want her caught." I can hear the anger in Nova's voice. She's a good and gentle person, but she believes in justice. "I googled the meaning of Rani's name," Nova says. "It means 'queen.'"

"And Queen Rani gets to decide who lives and who dies," I say. "Are you doing all right?"

Nova laughs softly. "As well as can be expected for a woman who's eight-and-three-quarter months pregnant and waiting for a call from a psychopath."

"Somewhere along the line, you must have made a bad life decision," I say.

"Actually, I've made quite a few bad life decisions," she says. "But none of them involved you. When it comes to you, Charlie, I have no regrets."

Through the glass that separates us, her eyes seek out mine. "Surprised?" she asks.

"Surprised and speechless," I say.

"You'll think of something." Nova glances at her computer screen, and her smile fades. "Charlie, take a look at your monitor. There's an email from someone named S.A. Viour."

"S.A. Viour," I say. "Saviour."

"Your Saviour," Nova says. "Read the note."

The message is chilling. *They're burying you, Charlie D. Every night*

they pile their weakness and lone-
liness and stupidity on you. They're
suffocating you. But it's almost over.
I'm going to save you. I'm going to
kill them all. After the first three,
it will be easy.

CHAPTER SIX

We've had gut-churning moments on the show before. Bomb scares from university kids who threatened to blow up the Lab Building so they wouldn't have to waste time studying for their finals. Suicide threats from people with pills. People with knives. People with guns. And people who knew how to tie a noose that would do the job. One night we even had a call from a guy lying on the subway tracks who said if we didn't tell the world what a witch his ex-girlfriend was, he was going to cuddle up with the third rail.

Amazingly, we've never lost a caller. We've come close. But somehow I've always been able to find the words that convince our lost souls that life is worth living. At least till we get off the air and Nova can connect them with a professional.

Tonight, my bag of tricks is empty and so am I.

Rani has killed three people. She's smart enough to know that her life is not going to have a happily-ever-after ending. The talkback is still open. "So where do we go from here?" I ask Nova.

She rakes her hair with her hands. "Beats me," she says. "I guess we just take care of business and keep the show moving. I'm going to play music for a while."

"We never just play music," I say. "I should go on air and explain."

"Explain what?" Nova says testily. "That we're playing music because there's a psycho out there killing our listeners?

45

In my opinion, it's better to have a hundred thousand people wondering why CVOX has suddenly become ALL MUSIC/ ALL THE TIME than to have a hundred thousand people going into cardiac arrest."

"You're right," I say. "But you're always right."

"No, I'm not," Nova says. "But I am right about this. Charlie, the police psychologist wants to talk to you directly. He's on line two. His name, incidentally, is Dr. Steven Apple."

"An Apple a day," I say.

"He doesn't like jokes about his name," Nova says. "I tried. He likes to be called Dr. Apple, and he'll call you Charlie—it's a power thing. Have fun."

I pick up the phone. "Charlie Dowhanuik here," I say.

"I'm Dr. Steven Apple." His bass voice rumbles with authority. Guys who are that certain of themselves make me want to scoop out their eyeballs with a spoon. But he's the only game in town.

"So, Steve, what's shakin'?" I say.

"Actually, it's Dr. Apple," he rumbles.

"Got it," I say. "So lay it on me. What do I do next?"

"You have to get Rani out of the shadows," he booms. "We have to know where she is, so we can keep her under surveillance."

I'm tempted to tell Steve that Emo Emily, with her screaming soul and her shoe fetish, could have figured that one out. But I need him too much to piss him off. "I'm doing everything I can," I say. "I just answered Rani's latest email. I told her she was right—that the pressure is too great. The walls are closing in. Unless I get help, I'm going to walk away again, and this time I might not come back."

"That's a very good start," Steve says. He sounds like my grade one teacher.

She always smelled of mint Life Savers and gin. I hang up and check out Nova's choice of music. The tune I'm listening to is Jann Arden's "I Would Die for You." Very tasty and very appropriate. I listen to Jann and stare at my computer screen. Rani is not answering my email. Steve calls. He believes that the reason Rani hasn't answered is that she's on the move. He thinks that she's on her way to her next victim.

"So we're screwed," I say.

He laughs his deep bass laugh. "Not at all," he says. "Rani's obsessed with your show. Even if she's on her way to commit murder, she'll tune in. She's the kind of listener you must dream about."

"Maybe I can get her to do a promo," I say. "So, doc, where do we go from here?"

"You go on the air and say everything you said in your email—pull out all the stops."

"Most of our listeners are hanging on by their toenails. If I say I'm desperate enough to pull the plug on 'The World According to Charlie D,' all hell will break loose."

"That's a chance you're going to have to take."

Nova surprises me by siding with the good doctor. So as Jann Arden sings the final lament of the doomed lover, I turn on my mike.

"This is for Rani. You're right. I'm suffocating, and I'm running out of time. I don't want to say goodbye to 'The World of Charlie D,' but I may not have a choice. I need to breathe. You've offered help. I'm asking for it now. Come down to CVOX, and Rani, hurry."

We go to music again. Three in a row. A record. But this is a record-breaking night. Our incoming call-board is twinkling like a Christmas tree, and the email inbox is jammed.

Nova calls me. "You've got to ratchet it up. The building is filled with cops, but they don't want to spook Rani, so they're staying out of sight. They're ready to take her, but they have no idea what she looks like, so they can't do anything until you get her inside the building. That's problem number one. Problem number two is our listeners. They're panicking, terrified that you're going to leave. And you know what happens when our listeners get scared. Charlie, you have to find a way to reassure them and still keep the heat on Rani." Nova's voice breaks. "Drat," she says. "Hormones. This is making me crazy. You're dancing on the edge of a razor blade, and there's nothing I can do."

"Sure there is," I say. "Be grateful I'm not wearing high heels."

Nova rewards me with a small laugh.

"I'll go back on the air and tell our listeners to hang with me," I say. "That should at least give us a little time."

"Do that. And Charlie, our old friend Marion the librarian is on line three. Take her call. Nobody can turn down the emotional temperature like Marion. Get her to unload some of her research—that'll chill everybody out."

"True enough," I say. "Marion's better than Xanax. Wish me luck." I flip on my mike and dig deep for my sane and hopeful voice. It's there.

"We're back," I say. *"And I'm doing better—not tip-top, but I'm still here. A glance out my nonexistent window tells me there's a full moon—always a lunar spookfest—so let's send back positive energy. Stay tuned and stay loose—we've got a lot of living to do."*

I start to cue the music, and I realize that tonight being cool is not enough. Our audience deserves more. When I start to speak again, the emotion in my voice is something I didn't put there. *"Thanks for hanging in,"* I say. *"Knowing you were there made all the difference."* My voice cracks. It's the real thing. I'm losing control, and it scares me.

CHAPTER SEVEN

I've fallen overboard, but lucky for me, I have a life preserver. I can hang on to Marion the Librarian until I'm paddling in safe waters again. I lean into my mike.

"You are listening to 'The World According to Charlie D' and our topic tonight is Erotomania. To help me navigate the tangled web of passionate longings and secret messages, we have an old friend: Marion the Librarian.

"Marion, my Marion, where have you been? I've missed the sound of your voice. I've become unmoored without your reassuring presence and your amazing breadth of knowledge."

"I've been listening, Charlie. And I've been calling, but your producer has been blocking my calls." Marion's voice is flat and angry. I don't blame her. We used her for a while. But when the network decided we had to go for a younger demographic, they drew up a list of callers who were no longer welcome. Marion's name was at the very top.

"You're on the air now," I say. *"And I'm going to put that Wikipedia brain of yours to work by asking a hypothetical question: If one of our listeners was the object of an erotomaniac's fixation, what should he or she do?"*

Marion leaps at the chance to share her expert knowledge. The chill melts. *"Call the police,"* she says earnestly. *"Do not—and I cannot emphasize this enough—do not attempt to handle the situation on your own. Only five percent of erotomaniacs kill. Most often they kill the 'triangulator'—that's the person whom they believe stands between them and the object of their love. But no one can predict what an erotomaniac might do. They are very, very dangerous. I repeat: Do not attempt to handle this situation on your own."*

"*Marion's advice is as solid as she is,*" I say. "*Pay attention to her words. If a lover you don't know is closing in on you, call the police. If you're obsessed with thoughts you can't control, call me. We can talk—off the air, if that's your comfort zone. I can put you in touch with somebody who can help. Whatever the problem—you're not alone.*" My eyes wander to my computer screen. No word from Rani. I look questioningly at Nova. She shakes her head to indicate that Rani is still a no-show.

Through the glass that separates us, I see that Nova is chewing her fingernails. She'd given that up, saying she didn't want to set a bad example for the baby. When I suggested that it would probably be a while before the baby cared about manicures, Nova rolled her eyes and told me there was a lot I didn't understand.

She was right. There is a lot I don't understand. But, ready or not, this seems to be my night for a crash course. Nova lays her head down on the desk. She looks so alone, and so vulnerable. Suddenly I know this isn't about me anymore. I lean into my mike. *"Rani, if you're listening, come down to the studio. So much depends on us seeing one another face-to-face."*

Marion cuts me off. "I'm *still here, Charlie,"* she says.

Her voice is stiff with fury. I blew it again. I'm off my game. *"I'm glad you're here,"* I say. *"Marion, my Marion, I need some help answering the big question about people who love this way. Why? Why do they do it? We all know that, sooner or later, even the greatest love will bring us grief. Why do erotomaniacs choose a love that brings them nothing* but *grief?"*

"That is the big question," Marion agrees. *"And it's a tough one. I've read up on this subject, and I think the writer C.S. Lewis has*

an answer for us. Someone once asked him why we love when losing hurts so much. He said we love so that we know we're not alone. Lewis's point is clear. For someone who has no intimacy in their life, even pathological love brings feelings of great joy."

"Even unrequited love is better than no love at all?" I say.

"That's it exactly," Marion replies. She sounds proud. I'm not the dunce in the class after all. *"Love gives people a reason to get up in the morning,"* she continues. *"The act of loving gives our life purpose."*

I lost the woman I loved three years ago. Sometimes, out of nowhere, I remember the care with which she folded her nightgown and placed it under her pillow. Or her insane joy when she beat me at Scrabble. And I can barely breathe. I can't remember the last time I wanted to get up in the morning. *"It's good to hear from you, Marion,"* I say, and my voice is choked.

I clear my throat and move along. *"You always have something worthwhile to say. People like C.S. Lewis give us perspective."*

Marion's laugh is short and dry. *"People don't care about C.S. Lewis anymore. They don't care about perspective. Listen to the people whose calls you take. They don't care about anyone but themselves. Me. Me. Me. Me. Me. That's all they care about. People who read and think are no longer relevant."*

I can hear the pain in her voice. She deserves to be heard. Our audience of demographically desirable young crazies should know there are people like Marion out there. People who may not be able to bare their souls on their blogs or on Facebook, but who are just as deeply wounded by life as they are.

"I've spent my whole life trying to find answers, and nobody cares," Marion says. *"My time is past. Nobody wants to hear from me. I'm too old, and I care about the wrong things.*

I'm obsolete. When you stopped taking my calls, you threw me on the scrap heap with all the other junk that people didn't need anymore. Televisions that aren't high definition, CD *players, portable radios, rotary phones. We're all garbage now. And we're all in the same burial ground."* Marion's voice catches. *"Charlie, I've been answering your questions. Now I have a question for you. How could you do this to me?"*

CHAPTER EIGHT

I can't answer. I didn't put up a fight when Nova told me the network wanted us to block Marion's calls. All I cared about was the show. If Marion got in the way of what the network wanted, she had to go. *"I'm sorry,"* I say. *"I mean that, Marion. I'm truly sorry."*

There's silence, and I think she's hung up. When, finally, she speaks, her voice is thick with tears. *"It's not your fault,"* she says. *"The world just passed me by."*

I glance into the control room. Nova is wiping her eyes. *"Marion, leave your number* with my producer," I say. "I'll call you after the show when we can talk privately."

"No," she says. Her voice is loud and frightened.

I'm confused. "If you'd rather I didn't call, I won't." For a beat, there's no sound on her end of the line. "Marion, would you rather I didn't call?"

Still no response. Then suddenly— there's a thud, a crash, the sound of glass breaking. I can hear Marion's voice, but it's distant. "What are you doing here?" she says. "How did you get in? The deadbolt was…"

I call out to her, "Marion, what's happening?" It's a stupid move. Marion's too far from the phone to hear me. And as an experienced caller, she knows enough to turn down the radio when she's on air. Suddenly the phone is slammed down. There's silence.

"What the hell's going on?" I say. I've forgotten to turn off my microphone. My question is echoing live from coast to coast.

Nova switches off my mike from the control room. She's on autopilot, but she's a pro. "Go to the tune," she says. "Script's on your computer screen. I've got the cops on the line."

I flick my button, and I'm back on air. *"Apologies,"* I say, *"but I take heart in knowing that my question was the question in all your minds.*

"In nine weird years, this is our weirdest night. Let's do what we can to keep our focus. Sarah McLachlan wrote a song about her stalker. It's called 'Possession.' Sarah's stalker sued her for using the material in the love letters he sent her. Later he blew off his head and sent Sarah the video." I pause to drive home the next point. *"No one's life should end like that,"* I say. *"Rani, call me."*

As Sarah sings about a man who would rather kill her than live without her, I call Nova. There's an edge in her voice, an urgency. "The police traced the number," she says. "Marion is one of theirs—a member of the police force. She's a researcher for their Major Crimes division. 'Marion the Librarian' was just your name for her. Her real name is Janet Davidson. She lives in a high-rise two blocks from here. The cops are on their way there now."

"So if Rani was there, she's close," I say.

"Very close. Charlie, the police think I'm a target because I'm the one who stands between you and her…"

"You're the triangulator," I say. "That's the term Marion used. Get out of here, Nova. Go home."

"Charlie, you know if I weren't pregnant, I'd stay. But I've waited so long for this baby."

"I know. Just go."

"The police are sending an officer to take me out of the building. They think I'm going to need protection for a while. They want you to stay on the air—appeal to Rani. Pull out all the stops. You have to get her to come to the station. The cops don't even have a description. Rani could be anywhere. She could be anyone. The one thing the police are certain of is that she's going to kill again." There's an edge of hysteria in Nova's voice. "Charlie, I have this...terrible feeling...that Janet Davidson is already dead. You have to do something."

"I'll give it my best shot."

"Be careful. If anything happened to you..."

"Nothing's going to happen to me," I say. "Only the good die young."

"You're good," Nova says. "You're one of the best people I know."

"You've got to start associating with a better crowd," I say.

She laughs softly. "When this is over, I'm going to teach you how to take a compliment. Charlie...hang on. The police say Rani's on line one. They want you to get her talking. An on-air confession will make things a lot easier for them."

"And for us," I say. "The network will love the publicity. We chose a wild and wacky business, Nova."

"I think the business chose us," Nova says. "My grandmother always said we have to grow where we're planted."

"Was your grandma ever faced with a psychotic serial killer?"

"I don't think so. She taught grade three. Look, my personal cop is waiting outside, so I'd better skedaddle. The police are covering the entrances to the building; there are three cops in the studio next to ours, and they're monitoring the show. If anything goes wrong, they'll be in. Now, reassure me. Tell me you're going to be all right."

"Mama Nova, I haven't been all right since the day I was born. Tonight the ride is just a little rockier than usual. Take care of yourself."

"You too, Charlie. You're very dear to me."

I reach for my tough-guy voice. "That goes both ways," I say. "Okay. Time for you and that baby you're carrying to let the boys in blue escort you home. Tomorrow morning this will all be over, and you'll have a truly rocking bedtime story to tell your daughter."

I watch as Nova throws her gear into her backpack. I figure she's heading out, but she surprises me by coming into the studio. She kisses my hair, murmurs, "Good luck," and then she's gone, leaving behind the scent of hemp oil. Someone told her it would prevent stretch marks.

The familiar smell boosts my spirits. I flick the button that opens my microphone. *"Rani, hello. I googled your name and learned that 'Rani' means 'queen.' What can I offer you that is worthy of a queen?"*

She growls, a low animal growl, and my marrow freezes. *"The beat of your heart,"* she says. *"The warmth of your arms. The press of your belly against mine. The electric thrill of your fingers running down the small of my back. I want to feel your body against mine."*

I try to match her intensity. *"Your voice is seductive, but words are just air, Rani. I need to see you, and you need to see me. Otherwise, how can we know what's real and what's fantasy?"*

"This is real," Rani shouts, and her voice is desperate. *"My feelings for you are real. Your need to be free is real. The parasites who are sucking you dry are real. They make demands, and you give in. I have to be the only one. That's why I'm clearing the field."*

"What do you mean 'clearing the field'?"

"Eliminating the ones in my way," she says. *"And that's not a fantasy, Charlie. That's real too."* Her voice becomes flat and weary. *"It isn't easy. It was at first, but now that the police have involved themselves, it's going to be tricky. I was lucky with the one I removed tonight. We have a mutual acquaintance.*

I was able to find out where she lives." Rani chuckles to herself. "*I guess it would be more accurate to say where she* lived."

"*Who was she?*" I ask.

"*That pathetic creature who drones on and on about her research…*"

My body goes numb. "*Janet Davidson,*" I say.

Suddenly Rani is spitting with fury. "*Don't you lie to me. You called her Marion. Marion the Librarian. That was her name. That was the name of the woman I eliminated.*"

I know the police are listening. They need a confession. "*What do you mean 'eliminated'?*" I ask.

"*Marion's gone,*" Rani says. There is no more silk in her voice. Her tone is steely. "*Marion had her chance to get a life…but she was always too fearful. She was a waste of skin, so I eliminated her. Take a deep breath, Charlie D. Fill your lungs with oxygen. For the first time in your life, you are living in a Marion-free universe.*"

CHAPTER NINE

The private line in the studio lights up. The caller ID says *APPLE*. It's my pal, Dr. Steve. I have a sense the news will not be good. Without explanation, I turn off my mike. "Make it quick," I say. "Rani's on line three."

"Keep her going." His voice booms with the finality of a church bell at a funeral. "An officer just called from Janet Davidson's apartment. It's a shambles. Books everywhere. Aquarium smashed and fish flopping on the floor. Ms. Davidson's bed has been slashed with a kitchen knife."

"What about Ms. Davidson?"

"She's gone. Vanished. Evidence of a struggle but no blood. Rani didn't have much time. The investigating officers think it's possible she knocked Janet Davidson out and has stashed her someplace in the high-rise. They think Janet is either dead or will be dead when Rani gets back to her. Charlie, it's imperative that you flush Rani out. She's the only one who knows where Janet Davidson is. This is our last chance to save a valued police officer."

"You've got it, Steve," I say. "One psycho coming up."

I flip my mike back on. *"Sorry,"* I say. *"Technical glitch. Rani, I have to see you face-to-face. I know you don't trust my producer. I've sent her home, so we can talk."*

"I need to be with you," she says. *"It's time."* Line three goes dead. I lean into my mike. *"We're moving closer to the midnight hour and that means we all drop our masks*

and let our real selves come out to play. Here's another variation on tonight's theme. Joni Mitchell and 'The Crazy Cries of Love.' Listen to the words, Rani, my queen, and fly to me."

The red light on the private line starts to blink again. I take off my earphones and throw them on my desk. I am tired of talking. I am tired of listening. I am just plain tired. I stare at the red light on the private line. Maybe it's my imagination, but the name *APPLE* on the ID seems to pulse like a neon sign, saying *Pay Attention to Me.* I ignore it. I've had enough.

"Crazy Cries of Love" fades down, and I'm back on air. *"You're listening to 'The World According to Charlie D,' and if I sound freaked, it's because I am freaked. But freaked or not, I forge ahead. Forgive any technical blips. My producer, Nova, left early. But whoa, here's a surprise! Nova is back in the booth with her escort for the evening."* I turn on the talkback. *"Mama Nova, why aren't you and that rather forceful-looking lady cop on your way home by now? My queen is undoubtedly on her way... you should not be here."*

Nova picks up the microphone from the desk. I'm baffled. She knows she just has to sit in her usual place to be heard. "Change of plans," she says. The female cop moves closer to her. This pleases me. I want Nova and her baby to be safe. "I need to be live," Nova says, and her voice is so tense it's almost unrecognizable. "We all need to be live," she says, and she spits the words.

I know immediately that something has gone terribly wrong. Nova is never on air, but when she says she needs to be "live," that's what she is asking for. Obviously, she wants the cops to hear everything she says. I flick on the mike in the control room and my own mike in the studio. *"So who's your friend?"* I say.

"This is Staff Sergeant Janet Davidson," Nova says tightly.

The relief washes over me. *"Janet Davidson! My own Marion the Librarian. Am I glad to see you."*

Nova's body jerks oddly, and she moves the microphone toward Marion.

"And I'm glad to see you, Charlie," Marion says. Nova's eyes meet mine. I see the terror on her face, and I understand it. Nova identified the woman with her as Janet Davidson. But the voice coming through the microphone isn't the flat, toneless voice of the police researcher whom I nicknamed Marion the Librarian. The voice in my earphones is low, seductive and unmistakable. It's the voice of Rani, Queen of the Air.

CHAPTER TEN

The woman standing behind Nova steps a little to the side. In the full overhead light, I can make out her general appearance. It's disturbing. She's heavy-set, middle-aged and dressed in a regulation-blue police uniform. She wears a cap with the force insignia. She looks like any other female cop. But there are two false notes. She's wearing makeup that is applied so heavily and awkwardly that it's almost clownish. And her cap is askew, allowing a number of platinum curls to escape. As I watch, the wig, of which the curls are a part, begins to slip to one side. Clearly Janet was in a hurry when she donned the wig, and she didn't have time to make the necessary adjustments. Keeping her left hand behind Nova's back, Janet grabs the microphone with her right. She puts her mouth too close to it, as amateurs always do. The closeness of the microphone distorts the voice, but the seductive growl is familiar.

"*I'm glad to see you, Charlie,*" she says. "*But there is no Janet. There is no Marion. There's just Rani now.*"

I can't get my head around it. The purring voice, the grotesque makeup, the wig, the curious positioning of Janet Davidson's body against Nova's.

"*She has her gun against my spine, Charlie,*" Nova says. "*I need to be live, Charlie. We all need to stay live. Help me.*"

"*I'm lost,*" I say. "*Janet…Rani. Why the gun? And how did Janet stop and you begin?*"

"*Janet was nobody,*" the curious creature

in front of me says. *"She was just a researcher for the Major Crimes Division. All day long she sat in front of her computer, analyzing other people's emotions: love, hate, envy, passion, greed, ambition. She became an expert on what drove the lives of other people. She had no life herself."*

"And that's why you...why she became Rani?" I say.

"That came later. At first everything was fine. Janet called your show because she heard that your topic was Nurture versus Nature. She'd read an article that said that the brain of a child who was ignored by his mother for the first two years of his life was different from the brain of a child who was lovingly nurtured. You probably don't even remember."

"I do remember," I say. "The lines were jammed after you—after Janet—called. Everyone had a story. It was a great show."

"At the end you thanked Janet, but as a joke you called her Marion the Librarian."

The seduction is gone from the voice of the woman in front of me. She sounds dead. *"You called her 'a pearl of great price.'"*

"And I said she should call me anytime," I say.

"That's exactly what you said." Rani's fury is back—hotter than ever. I see Nova's panic. *"Can you imagine what it meant to Janet to be invited into the life of a man like you? To know that, for the first time in her life, she was 'a pearl of great price'? Suddenly she had a reason to get up in the morning. As soon as she woke up, she would call your studio to find out the topic for that night. She would spend every coffee break, every lunch hour, researching the topic so she would have something to offer you. She lived for those calls."* Nova winces. Rani is jamming the gun into her spine. *"Then this person wouldn't let you take them anymore."*

"It wasn't Nova's choice," I say. "It's not her fault."

"*She took other people's calls. Young people. Twisted people. People who sounded…exotic.*"

"Charlie, please." When she calls my name, Nova's voice is forlorn.

Rani's face twists with rage. "*You sound desperate, Nova. Janet knew that feeling. Every time the show ended and you hadn't taken her call, she'd go into the bathroom, look in the mirror and then watch herself put the barrel of her gun in her mouth.*

"*A month ago, I…she almost pulled the trigger. She stared at her reflection for what seemed like hours. Then on the radio, she heard Charlie's voice. 'On the air, you can be anyone you want to be,' he said. That's when Janet knew that she could be the woman Charlie needed her to be—young, hot, great radio. The kind of woman whose calls would always be welcomed.*"

"And Rani was born," I said.

"*Every night Janet practiced the new voice in front of the mirror. It took a while, but it was* worth it. *When she closed her eyes and listened to the voice, she felt different—desirable, powerful. The voice was easy, but the face was harder. Janet bought the most expensive makeup in the city, but no matter how much makeup she put on, she was still old and plain. And you were perfect, Charlie."*

"I'm not perfect," I say.

She ignores me. *"Janet knew that a seductive voice might get her on the air, but she realized you'd never be satisfied with just a voice. You wanted a real flesh-and-blood woman. You deserved someone as perfect as you. She bought a very expensive wig. She was ready, but your lines were always jammed. Other people kept getting in the way. There were times when you talked to Ian Blaise twice in a single night."*

"He lost his wife and children," I say, and even as the words escape my mouth, I know I'm saying exactly the wrong thing.

Rani's wig slips down over her ear. She moves the microphone closer to her lips.

Her hiss is as venomous as a snake's. *"At least he had a wife and children to lose. Janet had never had anybody. Ian Blaise had memories…"*

"Marcie Zhang was only fourteen."

"And she'd already been rejected and laughed at. I did her a favor. I cut her pain short."

"But James Washington had everything ahead of him."

"And he still kept calling you. Don't you see, Charlie? Every minute you were on the air with James Washington, you weren't with me. I had to get him out of the way. It was nothing personal. He had to go, and now he's gone. And I'm here."

Nova is very pale. She sways as if she's about to collapse. Rani notices and grabs her roughly about the shoulder. The microphone is still in her hand and it knocks Nova's chin. She winces, but does not cry out. I've had enough. *"Let Nova go,"* I say.

My voice is louder than I intend it to be, and Rani tenses—the last thing we need. I try to be reassuring. *"Come into the booth with me,"* I say. *"We can do the show together. Nobody else. Just the two of us."*

Rani looks angrily at Nova. *"Your producer will never let me come in there. The minute I move away from her, she'll stop me."*

"I won't stop you. I swear," Nova says.

Rani adjusts her platinum wig. Under the mask of makeup, it's difficult to read the expression on her face, but her voice is resigned. It's the voice of a person who feels that events have been taken out of her hands. *"Of course, if Nova was dead,"* she says matter-of-factly, *"she couldn't stop me."*

CHAPTER ELEVEN

The control room is brightly lit. It's easy for me to see exactly what's happening. Nova is gripping the chair in front of her to keep from falling forward. From the angle of her arm, it's clear that Rani has the gun aimed at the base of Nova's spine.

Nova's voice is pleading. *"Just move the gun up, so it doesn't hurt the baby,"* she says. *"She hasn't done anything to you. Let her live... please. Please, Rani. If you're going to shoot me, okay, but please don't kill my baby."*

The jaws of the vice clamped to my temples tighten. The threat to Nova and her baby is more than I can take. *"Rani, we don't know how much time we have,"* I say. *"Let's not waste it. Nova has nothing to do with our lives now. She's the one who's irrelevant. Open the door to the studio and come to me."*

Rani hesitates. She and Nova are frozen, like figures on a TV screen when there's a transmission problem. My heart is pounding. Under my breath, I say, "Take the first step, Rani. You can do it. Take the first step. Once I get you in here with me, I don't care what happens as long as Nova and the baby are safe."

I lean into the mike. *"Rani, you know you want to see me. We've waited so long—too long. Come to me, Rani. Come to me. Come. Come."*

I watch the hands on the studio clock. It ticks off the seconds with agonizing slowness. Finally, Rani turns away from Nova, and like a sleepwalker she begins to move. I hate and fear guns, but I have never seen a more beautiful sight than the light glinting off Rani's Glock 22 pistol as she moves toward me. She raises the hand that is not holding the gun to straighten her wig and arranges her face in a tortured smile. When I'm certain Rani will not turn back, I allow myself to look at Nova. She is inching her way slowly toward the door that will lead her out of the control room to safety. For the first time since the show started that night, I exhale.

My relief doesn't last long. Within seconds, Rani opens the door to the studio. *"It's so dark in here,"* she says.

"That's how I like it," I say. *"Follow the sound of my voice."*

"I want to see your face."

"Do you?"

"I've imagined it a thousand times. I lie awake at night, touching your perfect body with my mind."

I reach for the light that I keep on the desk for an emergency and flick the switch. I tilt the lamp toward me, so that Rani can see my face clearly. She gasps. *"My god. What happened?"*

"I was born," I say. *"It's a birthmark. The human stain. Not the stuff of your dreams, huh?"*

Rani raises the gun, so that it's pointed at me. Despite her crooked platinum wig and her clownish makeup, she's a commanding figure. Her hand is steady as she takes aim. Behind her in the control room, I can see police officers moving into position. They, too, have their weapons drawn. I am beyond being frightened.

"You were supposed to be perfect," Rani says. *"We were supposed to be perfect."*

"And now you're going to shoot me because I'm not the man you wanted me to be."

"I killed for you."

"*No, Janet. You didn't kill for me. You killed for Charlie D. He only exists on the air. He's someone I made up because I didn't want to be me. Just the way you made up Rani because you didn't want to be Janet Davidson. My real name is Charlie Dowhanuik. Maybe it's time for Charlie Dowhanuik and Janet Davidson to meet.*" I stand and hold my arms out to her. "*You're going to have to put that gun down,*" I say.

With agonizing slowness, she places the gun on the desk. In the control room, the cops move into position. "*Give us a moment,*" I say. Janet Davidson moves toward me. I reach up and remove the wig. Her hair is short and brown. I touch it. "*You have pretty hair,*" I say.

She reaches out and touches my cheek. "*Your skin is very soft,*" she says.

"*Would you like to sit with me while I finish the show?*" I ask.

And so Janet Davidson sits down beside Charlie Dowhanuik. Facing us in the control room are six cops with their guns drawn. But until the program ends and the microphone is turned off for the night, the police are not a part of our world. The world of Charlie D and of Rani, Queen of the Air, goes far beyond this small dark room in the glass-and-concrete cubicle of CVOX radio. As long as the microphone is on, our world is the air. Our voices travel into rooms and minds and lives we can't even imagine. I turn to Marion. *"They're waiting,"* I say.

"Then help them," she says.

I smile at her and lean into the mike.

"You're listening to 'The World According to Charlie D,'" I say. *"It's March twentieth, the first day of spring, the season of love. Our topic tonight was love—the crazy things we do for love. So...lessons learned? I don't know.*

"I was born with a birthmark that covers half my face. It's still there. I'm a freak. I look as if I'm wearing a mask of blood. My mother told me that when the doctors and nurses saw me there was absolute silence in the delivery room. They handed me to my mother. She asked them to wash off the blood, but they told her nothing could take the stain away. Then my mother took me in her arms, kissed me and said, 'Then...we'll learn to live with it.'

"Maybe that's the lesson. Maybe we just have to learn to live with the stains that make us human. And you know what? It helps if there's someone who loves us enough to touch their lips to our imperfect bodies—to see the beauty in our imperfect minds.

"So be kind. As the poet says, 'There's a crack in everything. That's how the light gets in.' Put your arms around each other. Forgive one another for being human."

Janet smiles and reaches her hand toward mine. Our eyes lock and the split second of our communion is so intense that I don't notice she's picked up the Glock again. She aims it before I understand what's happening.

Janet may be a researcher, but she's also a cop. She was trained to know that the one place a shooter can be certain of achieving the desired result is the heart. There's a noise—surprisingly loud in our hermetically sealed world—a pungent odor that I learned from watching *CSI* is the smell of nitroglycerin, and then the hot sweet smell of human blood.

I look at my computer screen. One word: `Hallelujah`. It takes me a moment to realize that before she left, Nova keyed in the title of the last song for the night. I take a breath, lean into my microphone and announce the music that will take us out. *"Here's K.D. Lang singing Leonard Cohen's 'Hallelujah.' For those of you who are still with me, thanks for hanging in."*

I look at Janet. *"Not everybody made it,"* I say. *"Godspeed to those of you who had to leave. And Rani, Queen of the Air, keep flying."*

CHAPTER TWELVE

It takes time to clear a murder scene, but the cops are merciful. They lead Nova and me down the hall to the CVOX offices—well away from the stench and the sadness of Janet Davidson's death. They interview us separately. As I answer, I stare up at the photographs of the CVOX hosts that line the office walls. We are talk radio's heavy hitters. My photograph is a murky profile shot that shows only my good side. I decide that the next day, I'll get Nova to take a picture of me as I am. We'll get it blown up and hang it up for the world to see.

The police don't keep us long. They have most of what they need on the tapes of tonight's broadcast. The police officers are grave as they go about their business. I overhear two of them talking. Both officers had worked with Janet Davidson. They liked and respected her. Dr. Steven Apple, a gnome of a man with a carefully trimmed beard and hard-shined shoes, arrives and announces that he is there to counsel the officers through their grief. One of the cops who knew Janet Davidson tells Steve to take a long hike off a short pier. I give him two thumbs up.

When Nova and I walk outside, the air is sweet with the lilac scent of a soft spring evening. The breeze is gentle. Mick Jagger's tongue in the red-lipped mouth that forms the *O* in CVOX is blazing neon. Somewhere in the neighborhood, a junkyard dog bays at the moon. We are back in the known world.

Nova puts her hand in mine. Like children in a fairy tale, still haunted by the memory of a forest where every step led us deeper into darkness, we move quickly down the street. Past the shop that sells bargain wedding gowns. Past the pawnshops with the barred windows. Past the businesses that promise *Instant Ca$H for your Paycheck*. We reach the corner where Nova can catch the bus that will take her home.

At the bus stop, Nova tightens her grip on my hand. The sky is starting to grow light. We haven't spoken a word since we left the station. But we aren't ready to say goodbye. "I don't know about you," I say, "but I could use a cup of coffee. Fat Boy's is open."

Nova laughs and moves closer. "Fat Boy's is always open," she says. "Which is lucky because I have a hankering for a cherry coke and an order of onion rings."

"Breakfast of champions," I say. Then, still holding hands, Nova and I cross the street. We're walking east, into the sunrise, and toward the diner that prides itself on being the only place in town where, 24/7, the fun never stops.

RAPID READS

The following is an excerpt from
another exciting Rapid Reads novel,
The Barrio Kings by William Kowalski.

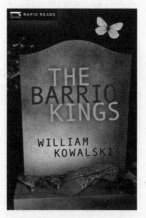

978-1-55469-244-6 $9.95 pb

"Look, man, real life is not always pretty.
Sometimes you gotta do hard things. You
have to protect what's yours in this life.
No one else will do that for you."

Rosario Gomez gave up gang life after his brother
was killed in a street fight. Now all he wants to do is
finish night school, be a good father and work hard
enough at his job at the supermarket to get promoted.
But when an old friend from the barrio shows up,
Rosario realizes he was fooling himself if he thought
he could ignore his violent past.

CHAPTER ONE

My name is Rosario Gomez. I'm twenty-three years old. I stock shelves at the supermarket downtown. I wear a tie to work every day, even though I don't have to. I wear a long-sleeved shirt to cover my tattoos. But I can't hide all of them. There's one on my right hand that says *BK* in small black letters. That one I can't hide. So I try to keep my right hand in my pocket when my boss is around.

My boss is Mr. Enwright. He's a fat, bald white guy who gets mad easy. But he's okay. Some of the other workers here call him Mr. Enwrong. I do not do that. Not to his face, and not behind his back. I need this job too bad. Enwright told me that once I get my GED he will promote me to assistant manager. That would be the most important job anyone in my family has ever had.

I was not always this straight. I came up rough. My neighborhood was on the news almost every night, and the news was never good. It was the kind of *barrio* nice people don't visit. There was nothing there for them. There was nothing there for me either. There was only survival, and I had to fight for that.

I dropped out of school to run with a gang called the Barrio Kings. I did some things I'm not proud of now. Like I said, I had to survive. I used to be the best street fighter around. I didn't like fighting. But I had no choice. I pretended to like it though. I used to smile. That scared people even more. And when you're scared, you lose.

Most fights are won before they start. You win them in your head, before you even throw a single punch.

I was just lucky that I was good at fighting, the way some people are just good at music or art. Sometimes I wonder if I should have been a boxer. But I always used to get this sick feeling in my stomach after I hit someone. It stayed with me. I don't miss that feeling. It's been a long time since I was in a fight. I hope I'm never in another one.

Things are different now. I've had this job for three years. I've stayed out of trouble. I don't go back to the old barrio anymore. I don't even miss it. Now I work from nine to five. After work, three days a week, I take the crosstown bus to the community college. That's where I take my night courses. I'm almost done with them. In just three weeks, I'm going to finish my high-school studies. Then I'll be the first person in my family to have a diploma too.

After class, I take another bus home. I live with my girlfriend, Connie. She's twenty. We've been together for two years. We're going to have a baby in a month. We already know it's a boy. We're going to name him Emilio. We have a crib all set up for him. We have a bunch of toys and clothes too. Connie's Aunt Carlita gave them to us. She has eight kids, so she has a lot of extra stuff.

By the time I get home after class, I'm wiped. But Connie has not been feeling too good lately, so usually I make dinner. I can't believe how big she is. Her feet hurt all the time. So do her hips and knees. I feel bad for her, but there's nothing I can do. And Emilio is almost here. I can't believe I'm going to be a dad.

Mr. Enwright told me that when I get that promotion, I will have to work longer hours, but I'll make more money. I can't wait. I have a plan. I'm going to save up money, and I'm going back to school. College this time. I'll take some business courses. I figure by the time Emilio is five, I can be a manager, and I will make even more money. That would put me on the same level as Mr. Enwright. I think Emilio will be proud to know his dad is a boss.

But I'm not stopping there. I want a business of my own. I don't know what kind yet. All I know is, I can see it in my head. Just like I used to see myself winning street fights. I can see myself in a three-piece suit. I'm not sitting in an office though. Who wants to sit still all day? Not me. I like to move around, talk to people, shake hands, make deals. I see myself in an airplane. I'm speaking different languages with people in other countries. Maybe I'll be selling things. Maybe I'll be setting up deals. Whatever it is, I'll be good at it. And I will make a lot of money.

But right now I need to come back down to earth. Mr. Enwright doesn't like it when people slack off. Not that I ever do. I just don't want to give him a reason to get mad at me. Not when everything is going so well.

Today is Thursday. That means I have class tonight. I hate riding that bus, but I can't afford a car right now. Cars are really expensive. You have your monthly payments, your insurance, your gas and repair costs. All that stuff adds up quick. And every penny I spend on a car means one penny less in the bank.

It doesn't matter about the bus. I don't mind. I do dream about a car though. I know just what kind I want. Not a low-rider, like I'm some kind of punk. I want a serious car. I want a black Lexus suv with a leather interior and tinted windows. I want people to look at that car and wonder who owns it. I want them to admire it. And it will have a nice stereo too. The kind you can hear a mile away.

CHAPTER TWO

It's Friday. I woke up early again. Connie was sore and needed me to rub her back. Man, I'm tired. But I don't complain. And I never slow down. Mr. Enwright never has to yell at me to move faster. Just today, he patted me on the shoulder and told me to keep up the good work. That promotion is waiting for me. All I have to do is earn it.

Five o'clock. My shift's over. I tell Enwright I'm leaving and head out the door. It's a warm day. I like the sun on my face. I wish I had more time to spend outside.

Maybe when Emilio is old enough, I can take him fishing. Or camping. I've never been camping, but I bet it's not that hard. Man, I cannot wait for that little dude to get here.

Suddenly I hear a whistle.

I stop. I know that whistle.

I look around, but I don't see where it's coming from. Maybe my ears are playing tricks on me.

Then I hear it again. This time I see where it's coming from. I can't believe it. Parked on the side of the street is a red El Camino. It's all tricked out, chrome everywhere. It has a stereo you can feel in your chest. And sitting at the wheel is a face I haven't seen in a long time. So long that I forgot all about him.

"Loco!" the face yells.

It's Juan. Who else would be calling me Loco? No one's called me that in a long time.

I walk over to the car.

"Juan? Is that really you?"

Juan turns down the radio.

"No, it's Elvis," he says.

"Man, it's been a long time."

"I know. Get in, bro."

"I gotta get home," I say. "Connie is waiting for me."

"Who's Connie?"

"My girlfriend," I say. "My baby mama."

"You a daddy?"

"Pretty soon."

"Come on, homes," says Juan. "I'll give you a ride."

That sounds pretty good. At least I won't have to ride the bus. So I ignore the funny feeling I'm getting in my stomach and get in.

"Look at you, man," I say. Juan is my age, but he looks a lot older. He lost some weight. A few new tattoos, not very good ones. His eyes are different too.

Colder and harder. I guess prison will do that to a guy.

Juan holds out his hand. He wants me to do the old handshake. At first I can't even remember it. He laughs at me.

"Look at you," he says. "You look like Mr. Clean. What happened to you? Where your colors at?"

"I don't wear the colors anymore," I say.

Juan looks like I just slapped him in the face. But he doesn't say anything. "Still got your wheels, I see," I say.

"My baby was in storage," he says. He runs his hand over the steering wheel. "I only got out yesterday."

"Who else you seen?"

Juan shrugs.

"No one special," he says. "I missed you, man. I didn't get no letters though."

"Ah, you know me and writing," I say. "It takes me forever."

"No phone calls? No visits?"

"I'm sorry, bro. I'm a busy guy. I got a good job. I'm gonna get a promotion. And I'm going back to school."

"Now I know you trippin'," Juan says. "School? What for?"

How do I explain my dreams to someone like Juan? He won't get it. He's been in the pen since he was eighteen. He probably doesn't even know how to write an email or use a cell phone. I could tell him about my business idea, but he'll just think I'm crazy. Suddenly the bad feeling in my stomach gets stronger. I wish I could just get out of the car and walk away. But something won't let me.

"You gonna drive, or are we just gonna sit here?" I say.

Juan starts up the car, and we pull out into traffic. He doesn't even look to see if anyone is coming. So he's still crazy. Great.

"I live up by the Hills now," I say. But when we come to the stoplight, he turns the wrong way.

"Where you going?" I ask.

"I just wanna take a drive," he says. "I ain't been behind the wheel for five years. I missed the road."

"I feel that," I say. I just hope he's not going to make me late. I have to make dinner again.

"So what's up with you?" Juan asks me.

"I just told you. Job, woman, baby, all that. That's what's up."

"I don't mean that."

"Then what?"

"How come you don't wear the colors anymore?"

"Man, don't you get it?" I say.

"No. Spell it out for me."

"I left the gang."

Juan looks at me like I just said I want to date his mother.

"What? You can't just leave the gang," he says.

"Well, I did."

"What for?"

"Man, how can you even ask me that? After everything that happened?"

"Yeah, but the Kings are forever," he says.

"I'm sorry you don't like it. But you were gone a long time. Things are different now."

Juan doesn't talk for a while. He just drives. Finally he says, "Can I ask you a favor?"

"What?"

"I need a place to stay."

I should have known that was coming. Connie won't like it. With her being so close to popping, she gets mad real easy at little things. She's not always like that. It's just hard being pregnant. I will never know what that's like, but I feel for her.

I feel for Juan too. He was my best friend once. He's got no one else. I can't tell him no.

"You can stay, but just for one night," I say. "Now get me home. I'm late."

CHAPTER THREE

Thanks to Juan, I get home half an hour late. That's not too bad. But like I said, Connie is really touchy these days.

We get out of the car. Connie's standing on the stoop, waiting. That is not a good sign. She only waits for me on the stoop when something is wrong.

Connie is the most beautiful woman in the world. She has long black hair and soft light skin. Her belly is as round as a basket-ball. On good days, her eyes are gentle. But today, they're full of fire.

"Where have you been?" Connie asks.

"Sorry, baby," I say. "I ran into an old friend. This is Juan."

"I was worried about you," she says. "Couldn't you have called?"

"Sorry," I say again. "I didn't mean it. Juan gave me a ride home."

"Wassup, *chica*?" Juan says. "Got a bun in the oven, I see."

"My name isn't chica," Connie says. "Rosie, who is this guy?"

"This is Juan. We grew up together," I say. "He's from the old barrio."

"Oh, great," says Connie. And without another word, she goes in the front door.

I turn to Juan.

"I know you been in prison a while," I say, "but you better watch your mouth."

"Whoa, easy," says Juan. "I was just trying to break the ice."

"You don't need to be breaking the ice. You wanna stay tonight, you just chill out. You feel me?" I say.

"I feel you, man," says Juan. "Relax. I'm cool."

We go upstairs. Connie didn't even leave the door open. I don't have my key, so I have to knock. She opens it after a minute. Then she goes right into our bedroom without saying anything. Man, is she mad.

I show Juan into the living room.

"Wait here," I say. "I'll be out in a minute."

"Good luck, homes," says Juan. He sits down on the couch and puts his feet up on the coffee table.

"Get your feet off there," I say. "I paid good money for that table."

Juan gives me a funny look. But he takes his feet off.

I go into the bedroom.

Connie's lying on the bed, on her side. She's facing away from me. I sit down and rub her back.

"You were supposed to make dinner for us," she says. She always says "us" now when she talks about herself. That's because she eats for two. I feel pretty bad. The baby must be hungry and kicking. Connie might get mad sometimes, but she never complains.

"I will. I just wanted to see how you were doing."

"Who is that guy?"

"I told you. Juan. An old friend."

"I never heard you talk about him before. Why is he here?"

"He's been away for a while," I explain. "He needs somewhere to stay."

"What? No way. Not in this apartment."

"Baby, please. Just one night. He doesn't have anywhere else."

"Why is that our problem?"

"It's not. I'm just being friendly."

"He was in prison, wasn't he?" says Connie. "I can tell by all that ink. He looks dangerous. What did he do?"

"He never did anything. He took a rap for somebody else."

"That's what they all say," Connie says. "Did he kill anybody?"

"No, Juan didn't kill nobody," I say. "Trust me, he's not going to hurt us. I already told him it's just for one night."

"Well, it better be," says Connie. "I don't want him to think this is a free hotel."

"All right, baby, listen. You just stay in bed. I'll make you some chicken and rice. You like that?"

"I just want some toast," Connie says. "I feel sick again."

"Okay. Be right back."

I close the door and go into the kitchen. I take some bread and put it in the toaster. Then I get out the butter. Juan is walking around, checking out our stuff. Our place is really small, but we're proud of it. We have a TV, a stereo, decent furniture. Connie keeps a picture of her mother on the wall, next to a statue of the Virgin Mary. She comes from a religious family. The living room and kitchen are like one room, with a counter between them. You can walk around the whole place in five seconds.

"Yo, man, what's for dinner? I'm starving," Juan says.

"You want some chicken?"

"Hells, yeah. Chicken would be great. You don't know what prison food is like."

And I never will, I think.

When Connie's toast pops, I cut it into triangles and take it in to her.

"Here, take a bite of this," I say.

She crunches her toast. Then she looks at me like she's been thinking.

"That guy, Juan," she says. "There's that one tat on his arm: *BK*."

"Yeah."

"You got the same one on your hand."

"Yeah. That's right."

"So he was in the Kings with you."

"Yeah, we were Kings together."

She chews her toast some more.

"Rosario, I'm gonna tell you this once," she says.

Uh-oh. She only calls me Rosario when she's really mad. Usually she calls me Rosie.

"What's that, baby?"

"You made me a promise. You remember?"

"Yeah, I remember."

"You still gonna keep it?"

"Of course, I'm gonna keep it."

"Because I need you. We got this baby coming. Right now, things are good. But it wouldn't take much to mess things up. You start banging again and everything goes out the window. Your job. This apartment. Me. The baby—"

I put my finger on her lips.

"Don't ever say that again," I say. "You and Emilio are my world. I would never do anything to mess things up. I promise."

"Okay," Connie says.

But I can tell she's not sure.

I'm going to have to prove it.

RAPID READS

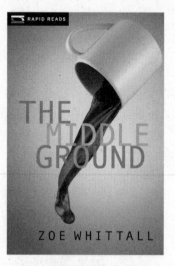

978-1-55469-288-0 $9.95 pb

When everything goes wrong at once, Missy Turner begins to make some unusual choices.

Missy Turner thinks of herself as the most ordinary woman in the world. She has a lot to be thankful for—a great kid, a loving husband, a job she enjoys and the security of living in the small town where she was born. Then one day everything gets turned upside down—she loses her job, catches her husband making out with the neighbor and is briefly taken hostage by a young man who robs the local café. With her world rapidly falling apart, Missy finds herself questioning the certainties she's lived with her whole life.

THE SPIDER BITES

MEDORA SALE

978-1-55469-282-8 $9.95 pb

"My name is Rick Montoya. But you can call me the Spider. Other people do."

When detective Rick Montoya returns to the city to try to clear his name after being accused of taking a bribe, he discovers someone is living in his apartment. Before he can find out who it is, the apartment house goes up in flames. Rick watches covertly as the police remove two bodies. Was the firebombing meant for him? Who exactly was killed in the fire? And why? What was his landlady Cheryl doing at home in the middle of the afternoon? And why is her daughter Susanna acting strangely? Then his estranged wife arrives at the scene of the fire. The questions mount up, along with the suspects.